"Not Me!" Said the Monkey
Copyright © 1987 by Colin West
First published in England by Walker Books Ltd, London
All rights reserved. No part of this book may be used
or reproduced in any manner whatsoever without written
permission except in the case of brief quotations
embodied in critical articles and reviews.
For information address Harper & Row Junior Books,
10 East 53rd Street, New York, N.Y. 10022.
Printed in Hong Kong by Sheck Wah Tong Printing Press Ltd.
First Harper Trophy edition, 1989

Library of Congress Cataloging-in-Publication Data
West, Colin.
    "Not me!" said the monkey.

    Summary: A mischievous monkey causes trouble for all
the other animals in the jungle but denies it to the end.
    [1. Monkeys—Fiction.   2. Animals—Fiction.
3. Jungles—Fiction]   I. Title.
PZ7.W51744No 1988   [E]   87-3712
ISBN 0-397-32253-4
ISBN 0-397-32254-2 (lib. bdg.)

    "A Harper Trophy book."
ISBN 0-06-443167-3 (pbk.) 87-8417

"NOT ME!" SAID THE MONKEY

WRITTEN AND ILLUSTRATED BY

Colin West

A Harper Trophy Book

Harper & Row, Publishers

"Who keeps walking all over me?"
hissed the snake.

"Not me," growled the lion.
"And not me," said the monkey.

"Who keeps throwing coconuts about?" snorted the rhino.

"Not me," hissed
  the snake.
"Not me," growled
  the lion.
"And not me,"
  said the monkey.

"WHO KEEPS TICKLING ME?" roared the elephant.

"Not me," snorted the rhino.
"Not me," hissed the snake.
"Not me," growled the lion.

"And not ME!"
said the monkey.

Slurp! Slurp! Slurp!
went the elephant.

WHOOOOOSH!

"Now who's going to stop all this monkey business?" laughed the lion, and the snake, and the rhino, and the elephant.

"NOT ME!"
said You-Know-Who.